And Pigs Might Fly!

Michael Morpurgo
and Shoo Rayner

Jessy Runs Away · Best Friends · **Rachel Anderson**
Weedy Me · **Sally Christie**
Two Hoots · Almost Goodbye Guzzler · **Helen Cresswell**
Magic Mash · Nina's Machines · **Peter Firmin**
Shadows on the Barn · **Sarah Garland**
Clever Trevor · **Brough Girling**
Private Eye of New York · **Nigel Gray**
Desperate for a Dog · Houdini Dog · **Rose Impey**
Free With Every Pack · The Fizziness Business ·
Cowardy Cowardy Cutlass · Mo and the Mummy Case ·
Robin Kingsland
Mossop's Last Chance · Albertine, Goose Queen ·
Jigger's Day Off · And Pigs Might Fly! · **Michael Morpurgo**
Hiccup Harry · Harry's Party · Harry with Spots On ·
Chris Powling
The Father Christmas Trap · **Margaret Stonborough**
Pesters of the West · **Lisa Taylor**
Jacko · Rhyming Russell · **Pat Thomson**
Monty, The Dog Who Wears Glasses · Monty Bites Back ·
Monty – Up To His Neck in Trouble · **Colin West**
Ging Gang Goolie – It's An Alien! · **Bob Wilson**

Published 1991 by A & C Black (Publishers) Limited
35 Bedford Row, London WC1R 4JH

Text copyright © 1991 Michael Morpurgo
Illustrations copyright © 1991 Shoo Rayner

ISBN 0 7136 3488 X

A CIP catalogue record for this book
is available from the British Library.

Filmset by Kalligraphic Design Limited, Horley, Surrey
Printed in Great Britain by William Clowes Ltd, Beccles, Suffolk

Chapter One

There was once a family of all sorts
of animals that lived in the
farmyard behind the tumble down
barn on Mudpuddle Farm.

At first light every morning
Frederick, the flame-feathered
cockerel, lifted his eyes to the sun
and crowed and crowed
until the light came
on in old Farmer
Rafferty's
bedroom
window.

Ah sweet mystery of light, at last I've found you...

One by one the animals crept out into the dawn and stretched and yawned and scratched themselves. But no one ever spoke a word—not until after breakfast.

Old Farmer Rafferty put in his teeth, looked out of his bathroom window and shook his head.

And he opened the window and shouted,

Go away, sun! You hear me? Run off and shine somewhere else. Go on, push off!

But the sun was too far away to hear. It just went on shining.

Chapter Two

Out in the farmyard the animals looked up at the sun and sighed.

So they all put their hats on, except for Egbert the greedy goat who had already eaten his –

and Pintsize
who thought pigs looked silly in
hats. But then Pintsize *never* did
what he was told.

9

Down at the pond Upside and
Down, the two white ducks that no
one could tell apart, had their heads
stuck in the mud because there was
hardly any water left in the pond.

Albertine sat still as a statue on her
island, shading her goslings under
her great white wings.

'When's it going to rain, Mum?'
they peeped.

'Sometime,' she said, and she
settled down to sleep because it was
the wisest thing to do and Albertine
was the wisest goose that ever lived
(and everyone knew it, including
Albertine).

So, thirsty and dusty and itchy, the animals trooped down to ask her advice, all except Mossop, the cat with the one and single eye, who was fast asleep on his tractor seat.

I haven't had a bath for weeks, nor have my babies.
You're a fine one to talk.
We know.... we can smell you know!
Now now, no quarrelling!

said Diana the silly sheep.

'What about you?' said Jigger, the almost-always sensible sheepdog.

Frederick looked up at the buzzards and larks and swifts and swallows. 'If only I could fly like them. Must be cool up there,' he sighed.

And little Pintsize looked up too and thought just the same thing.

15

'You've got wings,' said Egbert.
'Use them.'

'Now, now,' said Captain. 'We're quarrelling again.' And he called out to Albertine.

So that's what they all did –
Captain in the darkest corner of his
stable,

Jigger under the
rhubarb leaves in
the vegetable patch,

Aunty Grace and Primrose side by
side under the great ash tree,

Egbert behind a pile of paper sacks
in the barn so he could be near his
lunch,

and Diana right in
the middle of the
sunniest field
because she was
very very silly!

Frederick went wherever his
speckled hens did – and as they all
went in different directions, he
found that very difficult!

While Peggoty and her little pigs, including Pintsize, crawled into a patch of nettles and lay still. Soon all the animals were fast asleep . . .

except Pintsize who wasn't at all sleepy.

20

Chapter Three

Of all Peggoty's little pigs Pintsize
was definitely the naughtiest. Say
'do this' and he'd do that. Say 'come
here', and he'd go there. It was just
the way he was. Some children are
like that.

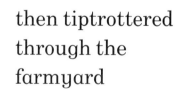

He waited until
Peggoty was snoring,

then tiptrotted
through the
farmyard

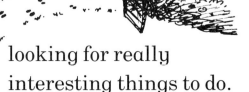

and down the
lane

looking for really
interesting things to do.

21

He hadn't gone far when he saw old Farmer Rafferty leaning on a gatepost and talking to the next-door farmer. Both of them were gazing up at the sky.

Cows are lying down. Sure sign of rain. It's coming, I can smell it.

Farmer Rafferty shook his head as he squinted at the sun.

he said,
and he laughed like a drain.

Pintsize pricked up his ears, (which
isn't easy for a little pig).

And he jumped up and down
in wild excitement.

23

I'm a pig.........
So that means.....
I can fly!.....
Yipeee!.........
I can fly!.....
I can fly!.....
What's the matter with that little pig of yours?
Too much sun I expect.
How about a nice glass of lemonade?
Yes Please.

Chapter Four

Flying was not nearly as easy as it looked. Pintsize stood up on his back trotters and flapped his front ones – trotters, he thought, would do just as well as wings.

But however hard he flapped (and flapping trotters is *not* easy) and however much he jumped up and down, he somehow never managed to take off. But Pintsize was not a giving-up sort of pig. He sat down and thought about it.

Nothing's ever easy at first. I mean, it took me days before I could walk. What was it Mama said to me? Practice makes perfect.

He was out in the meadow, practising his trotter flapping, when a crow spotted him and landed beside him.

What are you up to little piggy thing?

I'm learning to fly.

We've got a right one here!

The crow cackled and flew off to tell
his friends, then they all cawed
together until they got sore throats
– which served them right.

Suddenly Pintsize had an idea.

Upside and Down,
they can fly.
I've seen them.
They'll teach me.

And he trotted off down to the muddy pond. 'Upside! Down!' he squealed, but they couldn't hear him, not with their heads in the mud.

UPSIDE! DOWN!

Shhh!

Hush!

Sorry!

Quiet

BLUB

GLUG

In the end he got a long stick and poked

Upside in his down,

and Down somewhere else!

They were not at all pleased.

'What, like this?' they quacked.
And they took off and looped a loop.

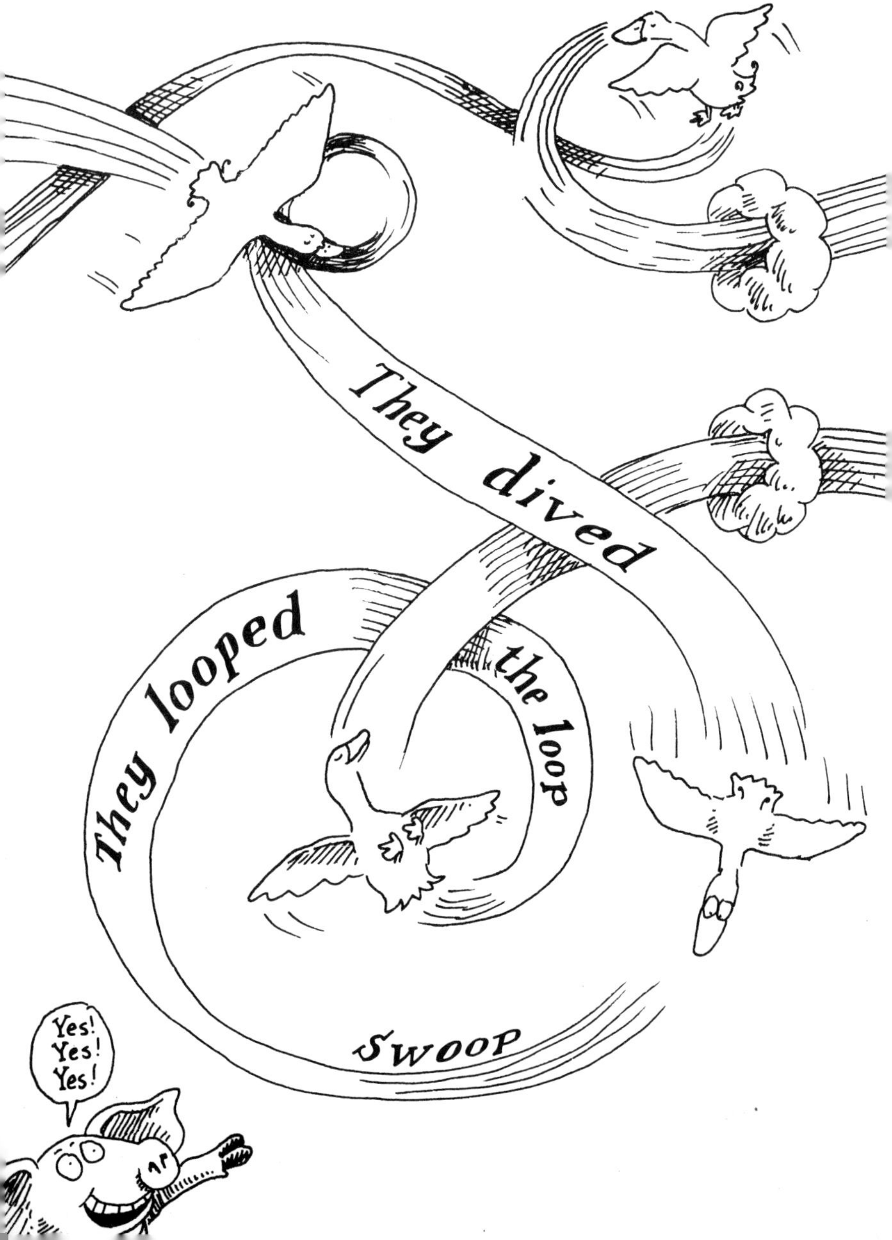

They dived

They looped

the loop

swoop

Yes!
Yes!
Yes!

They floated

Wooosh!

They soared

They landed quite puffed. 'Like that?' they quacked.

'Yes,' said Pintsize. 'Just like that.
Please teach me. *Please.*' But they
sniggered and snickered as ducks do.

'Just you watch me,' said Pintsize,
and he climbed up the garden wall,
took a deep breath and then ran . . .

until suddenly there was no more
wall to run on . . . and he was flying
through the air!

32

For one wonderful moment he was
up there with the birds, but then
something was pulling him down and down and down and he was turning over and over . . . .

Then he landed,

in the muddy pond.

'Oh dear,' thought Albertine. 'I suppose I'd better do something about this.'

So she stood up and honked and
honked until all the animals woke
up and came running.

Pintsize was climbing the ladder (and that's not easy if you're a pig) up onto the haystack.

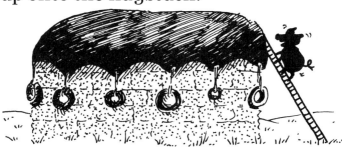

Peggoty closed her eyes, 'I'm not looking,' she said.

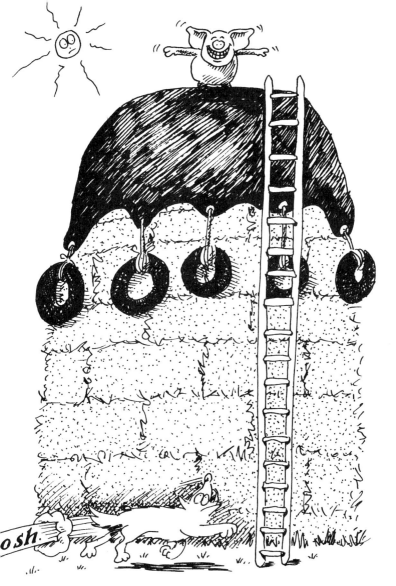

Jigger sprinted across the farmyard
until he was standing right under
the haystack. 'Don't jump!' he barked.
'Don't do it' . . . But Pintsize did it.

For one wonderful
moment he was
up there with the
birds, but then
something was
pulling him down
and down and
he was turning
over and over,
and then he landed –

SQUOOOOOF!

on Jigger's back.

Jigger never knew
that little pigs
could be that heavy.
But he knew now.

And very soon they all knew,
because wherever Pintsize went
they had to go, so that whenever he
jumped, one of them was always
there for him to land on.

Every time he jumped he flew
further – or he thought he did, 'I can
fly,' he'd squeal. 'Pigs can fly.'

And it was true – well, sort of.

Pintsize flew as far as a pig ever had
flown, but then he'd drop like a
stone and knock all the air out of
poor Aunty Grace
(and that's
a lot of air),

or Primrose

or Captain

or Egbert

or Frederick.

But the one he liked landing on
most was Diana, because she was
very soft and very springy and very
spongy.

'Thanks, Diana,' he'd squeak and off he'd go again before anyone could catch him.

This can't go on.

You can say that again.

This can't go on.

I've tried everything I can, he just won't listen to me.

Something's got to be done.

Too true, quite right.

But what?

Everyone looked at Albertine to see if she'd had one of her ideas.
And of course she had.

'Don't you worry,' she said. 'I'll have a word with a friend of mine. I've got friends in high places you know. Just you keep your eye on Pintsize, all of you.'

Chapter Five

Drooping in the heat of the day, the animals did as Albertine said and trailed around the farm after Pintsize. They found him teaching his brothers and sisters. Standing up on his back trotters, Pintsize was explaining how a pig flies.

'You just wave these,' he said,
flapping his front trotters, 'and you
lift off. Simple when you know how.'

And all the little pigs stood up and
waved their front trotters.

While she wasn't looking, a buzzard
flew down and landed beside
Pintsize.

'Am I ready?' said Pintsize. 'Course I'm ready!' And before he knew it, the buzzard had picked him up and was soaring into the sky high above the farm.

‘Nice view,’ said the buzzard.

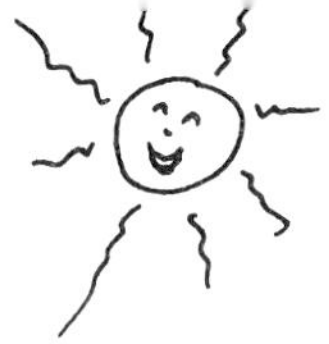

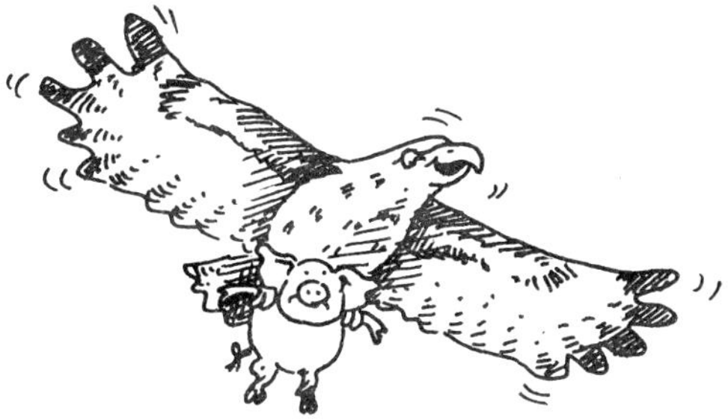

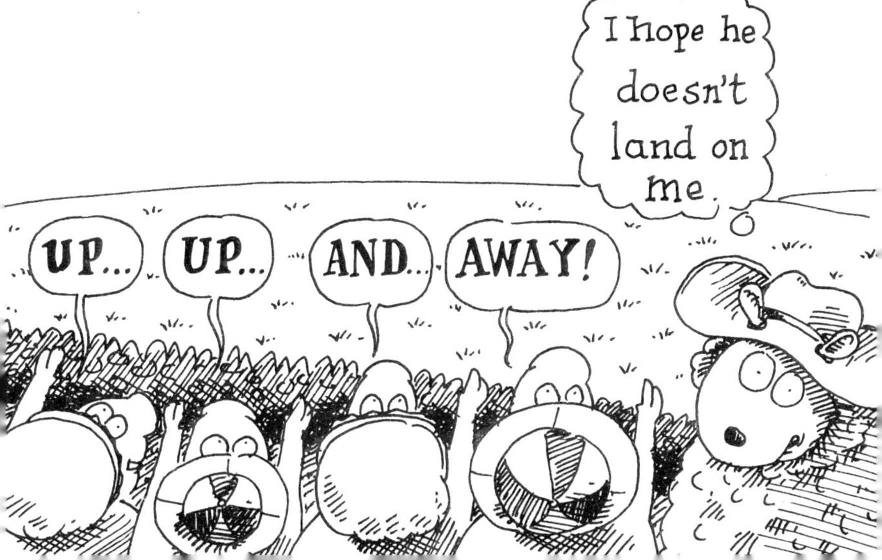

Pintsize looked down, and wished he hadn't. His stomach started to turn over and he began to feel very sick and very frightened. The animals below him were getting smaller

and smaller.

Then he couldn't see them any more.

49

'Take me down,' he squealed. 'Take me down.'

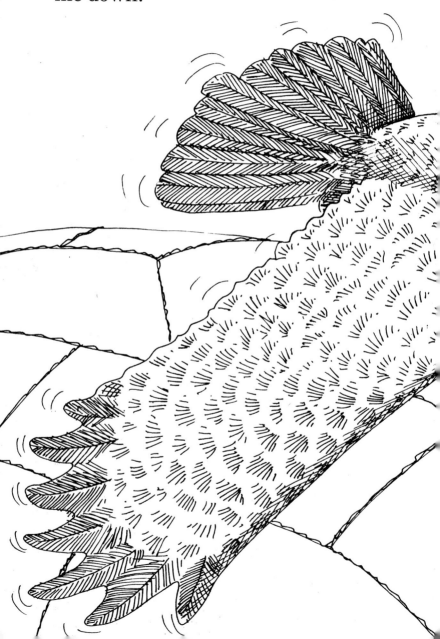

Pintsize tried to scream, but he couldn't. He was so frightened he couldn't even breathe . . .

The farm was coming closer and closer, it was getting bigger and bigger! He was going to crash!

Pintsize closed his eyes.

Putt
Putt
Putt
...ON ...ON
Please take me home....Please.....
WWOOOOOOOOOSH...
Like flying do you?
Pintsize has got the hang of it now.
Great idea Mum.
I know.

'Not yet,' said the buzzard, and as they floated through the silent sky they came to a cloud, a dark cloud. 'Don't like the look of that,' said the buzzard a bit louder than he should.

Thunder rolled around the sky and the rain began to fall in great dollops.

'I want to go home,' squealed Pintsize. 'I want my mama.'

'All right,' said the buzzard, 'I'll drop you off.'

And he did just that!

Down below, Farmer Rafferty was talking to the next-door farmer again.

'Yippee! Yarroo!' cried old Farmer Rafferty, and he did a sploshy rain-dance in a muddy puddle. But if he hadn't been so busy dancing, he'd have noticed that it wasn't raining cats and dogs at all – it was raining pigs. And one little pig in particular!

Pintsize tumbled through the air until at last he landed right in the middle of the ....

DUNG HEAP

'Yes, Mama,' said Pintsize – and he
meant it. He snuggled into her and
buried his head in the dung so he
couldn't hear the thunder.

That evening Jigger saw Albertine
as she was having her bath.

'Maybe,' said Albertine and smiled
her goosey smile.

Meanwhile ....

On his tractor seat, Mossop
woke up.

61

Peggoty put her trotters over Pintsize's ears so he couldn't hear any more.

'If you insist,' sulked Mossop and he yawned hugely as cats do, closed his one and single eye and slept.

The night came down, the moon came up and everyone slept on Mudpuddle farm.